This book belongs to

....

Retold by Ronne Randall
Illustrated by Anna C. Leplar

This is a Parragon Publishing Book
First published in 2006

Parragon Publishing
Queen Street House
4 Queen Street
Bath BA1 1HE, UK

Copyright © Parragon Books Ltd 2006

ISBN 1-40545-123-8
Printed in Indonesia

The Grimm Brothers

Little Red Riding Hood

p

There was once a little girl who lived with her mother at the edge of the forest. She was kind and sweet, and everyone loved her.

On the other side of the forest lived the little girl's granny. Granny looked forward to her granddaughter coming to visit, and always gave her a present.

The very best present was a riding cape, with a hood, made of red velvet. The little girl liked it so much that she wore it all the time. So everyone called her Little Red Riding Hood.

One day, Little Red Riding Hood's mother put some cake and fruit in a basket.

"These are for Granny," Mother told Little Red Riding Hood. "She isn't feeling well, and these goodies will cheer her up and help her get better."

"I'd like to help Granny get better!" said Little Red Riding Hood. "Can I take the goodies to her?"

"Of course," said Mother. "But you must promise to be very careful on your way through the forest. Stay on the path, and don't speak to ANY strangers!"

"I promise, Mother," said Little Red Riding Hood, and off she went.

As Little Red Riding Hood skipped along the path through the forest, she didn't know that a sly, greedy old wolf was watching her from behind a tree!

When she was just a little way down the path, the wolf sprang out in front of her.

"Good morning, my dear!" said the wolf, with a big, toothy grin.

Little Red Riding Hood remembered what her mother had told her, and she didn't speak to the wolf. She kept walking straight down the path. But that sly old wolf just followed her!

"I can see what a kind girl you are," said the wolf. "Won't you wish me a good morning?"

Now, Little Red Riding Hood was kind and sweet. So she stopped for just the tiniest moment and said, "Good morning, sir."

The sly old wolf smiled a very wide smile, thinking what a sweet, tasty snack Little Red Riding Hood would make. "Where are you going on this fine morning?" he asked.

Not wanting to be rude, Little Red Riding Hood answered, "To my granny's house, on the other side of the forest, sir. She isn't feeling well, and I'm taking some goodies to cheer her up."

"Hmm," the wolf thought to himself. "This little girl might make a sweet snack, but her granny would make a tasty meal!" He began to work out a crafty plan.

"Wouldn't your granny like some pretty flowers?" the wolf asked Little Red Riding Hood. "There are so many growing near the path!"

"Yes, Granny loves flowers," said Little Red Riding Hood. "A pretty posy would help cheer her up!"

Little Red Riding Hood began to gather the flowers growing near the path. But soon she forgot her mother's warning not to stray from the path. She strayed farther and farther into the forest, finding all the very prettiest flowers for Granny.

Meanwhile, the wolf hurried to the other side of the forest and went straight to Granny's house. He tap-tapped lightly on the door.

"Who's there?" called Granny.

"It's Little Red Riding Hood," called the wolf, in his softest, sweetest voice. "I've brought you a basket of goodies!"

"Just lift up the latch, open the door, and come in," said Granny.

So the wolf lifted the latch…opened the door…and went right in.

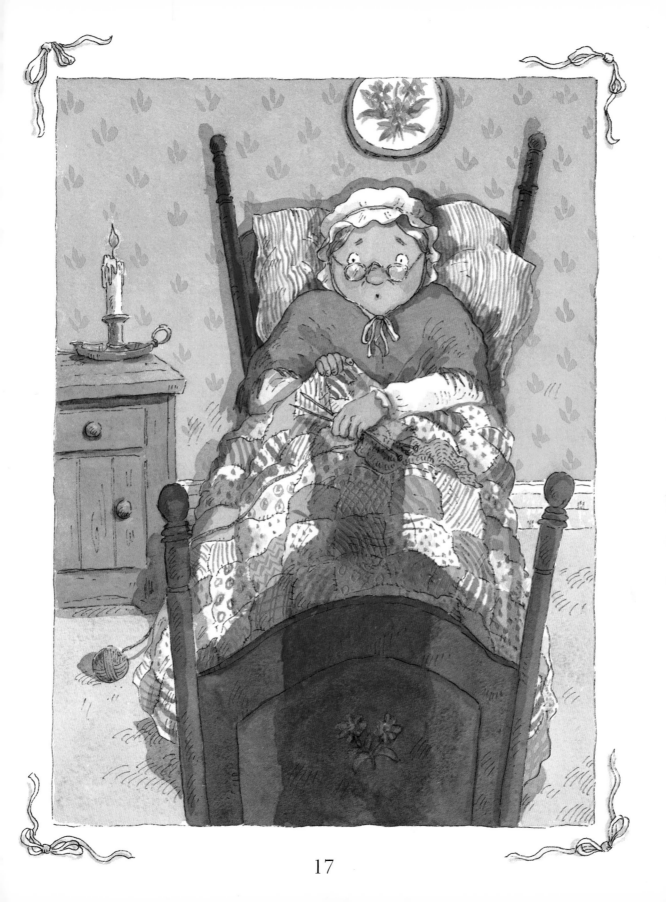

Before poor Granny even knew that it was the wolf, he had gobbled her up in one big gulp.

Then he put on her nightcap and crept into her bed with the covers tucked under his chin.

"I'll have the little girl for dessert!" he said to himself with a big, toothy grin.

A little while later, Little Red Riding Hood arrived at the cottage with a pretty posy of flowers. She tap-tapped lightly on the door.

"Who's there?" called the wolf in his gentlest granny voice.

"It's Little Red Riding Hood," she replied. "I've brought you a basket of goodies!"

"Just lift up the latch, open the door, and come in," said the wolf.

So Little Red Riding Hood lifted the latch, opened the door, and went right in.

Little Red Riding Hood looked over at the bed.

"Poor Granny must be very ill," she thought. "She looks so strange!"

She stepped closer to the bed.

"Oh, Granny!" she gasped. "What big eyes you have!"

"All the better to see you with, my dear," said the wolf. Little Red Riding Hood stepped even closer.

"Oh, Granny!" she said. "What big ears you have!"

"All the better to hear you with, my dear," said the wolf. Little Red Riding Hood stepped right up to the bed.

"Oh, Granny, what big hands you have!"

"All the better to hold you with!" said the wolf.

"Oh, Granny!" she said. "What big teeth you have!"

"All the better to eat you with!" growled the wolf, jumping out of bed. And he gobbled up Little Red Riding Hood in one big gulp!

With his belly so full it was almost ready to burst, the wolf lay back down on the bed and fell fast asleep.

At that moment, a hunter was passing Granny's cottage, and he heard a strange sound coming through the open window.

"The poor old woman is snoring very loudly!" the hunter said to himself. "I'd better go in and see if she's all right."

So, in went the hunter. Of course he saw that it wasn't Granny who was snoring at all—it was the wolf!

"I have been hunting you for a long time," he cried. "Now, at last, I have found you!" He raised his gun to shoot the wolf. But then he looked at the wolf's belly.

"You sly old wolf!" cried the hunter. "From the size of your belly, I'd say you've swallowed poor old Granny!"

He took out his hunting knife and very carefully slit open the wolf's belly—zip, zip!

Out jumped Granny—and Little Red Riding Hood, too!

"Thank you for saving us!" said Granny.

"It was so dark and horrible in there!" said Little Red Riding Hood.

While the wolf was still asleep, Little Red Riding Hood went outside and got some stones. She brought them in and filled the wolf's belly with them. Then the hunter stitched up the wolf's belly as good as new.

When the wolf woke up a little while later, he had such a bellyache that he ran out of the cottage moaning and groaning. He went off to hide in a cave, and was never, ever seen again!

As soon as the wolf was gone, Little Red Riding Hood and Granny sat together to enjoy the basket of goodies. Before long, Granny was feeling much better.

Little Red Riding Hood said, "As long as I live, I will never leave the path and run off into the woods by myself if Mother tells me not to." And she never did.

The End